A

As you'd expe........ ...., Hugh
Scott has always been fascinated by ghosts and
the supernatural. "I like spooky things," he says.
"I grew up reading ghost stories, listening to
them on the radio and I've had some creepy
experiences of my own." It's no wonder then that
he writes spine-chilling stories himself.

It was in 1984, two years after winning the
Woman's Realm Children's Story Writing Com-
petition that he decided to give up his job as an
art teacher and become a full-time writer: "I had
this feeling inside me, just sitting in my solar
plexus – a little diamond of pure knowledge, very
hard and strong, and I knew it wouldn't go away
until I left teaching and became a writer." His
first novel, *The Shaman's Stone*, was published in
1988 and several more titles soon followed.
These include *Why Weeps the Brogan?* (Winner
of the 1989 Whitbread Children's Novel Award),
*Something Watching, The Gargoyle, A Box of
Tricks, The Place Between, The Camera Obscura,
Freddie and the Enormouse* and, most recently,
The Ghosts of Ravens Crag.

Hugh Scott is married with two grown-up children and grandchildren and lives in Scotland.

Other books by Hugh Scott

For younger readers

Freddie and the Enormouse
The Summertime Santa

For older readers

A Box of Tricks
The Camera Obscura
The Gargoyle
A Ghost Waiting
The Place Between
The Shaman's Stone
Something Watching
Why Weeps the Brogan?

A BOX OF TRICKS

HUGH SCOTT

WALKER BOOKS
AND SUBSIDIARIES
LONDON · BOSTON · SYDNEY

*This story is for
Aunt Nancy
who would have been pleased*

First published 1991 by Walker Books Ltd
87 Vauxhall Walk, London SE11 5HJ

This edition published 1996

2 4 6 8 10 9 7 5 3 1

Text © 1991 Hugh Scott
Cover illustration © 1996 Bruce Pennington

Printed in Great Britain

British Library Cataloguing in Publication Data
A catalogue record for this book is available
from the British Library.

CONTENTS

PART ONE

PART TWO

PART ONE

A VERY ODD HOUSE!

The sun shone, hot as a fried egg, across the fields.

Above the stream, the shadows of trees sparkled with insects.

"We can't paddle in that!" complained Maggie, and the insects shifted at the crack of her voice. But she tugged off her sand-shoes anyway, and stepped into an ankle-high waterfall. Her hair dangled like folds of melting butter as she peered at her toes.

"It's freezing!" she yelled.

"We should get back," said John. "Aunt Nell — "

"Nellie can jump off the roof!"

"You know she'll be hurt if we're inconsiderate – "

"Oh, and walk about with nose up and her bottom out! I'm *coming!* I can't stand her silences!"

Maggie sat on a rock, bare legs everywhere as she struggled into her sand-shoes. "Race you to the card table!"

She scrambled up the bank, hair flying.

John followed, not racing.

He burst from the trees into sunlight, where the meadow dozed beside the stream – which would have been a river, if the sun had allowed any rain to fall. He trotted after Maggie.

A nettle sting burned above his knee, so while he trotted he looked for dock. He saw it, and ripped away a leaf, crushing the leaf, hoping for juice, holding it on the sting. He sprawled joyfully in hard grass.

"Come on, Slowcoach!" rose from the bottom of the meadow, where Maggie was using a five-bar gate as a stepladder, bouncing on her toes.

He dropped the dock, and jogged easily, skipping against stones, sending them leaping from his feet in puffs of dust. The dying stream gurgled beside him.

Maggie stepped from the gate, and they battered the path under their sand-shoes as they raced the last hot paces.

They sprawled, backs cool on the card table; cool, for the table was white marble, and not a table at all, but a quaint tombstone that had amazed John and Maggie when they first saw it. The top slanted from the ivy-covered ground, because two legs were broken. Marble cards and marble guineas on the table seemed ready to spill – but they never would.

John twisted onto his knees and his fingers found the card player's name, Simon Welkin, cut round the table's edge. More words vanished under ivy that rustled with dust and spiders.

Beyond the table spread a flat garden, thick with vegetables, heavy with plum trees and crab apple. A duck, fat as a snowman, struggled up from the stony bed of the stream; and the house was quite the strangest John had ever seen.

It had once been a church, but the ground had softened, and sucked the building down, leaving the window-sills level with the earth. Steps had been dug to let people under the decorated archway of the main door. And many grim carved faces lay smothered in the garden, for the tower had tilted, dropping stones, and the tower seemed, in the blaze of evening sunlight, to peer at the ground in search of its lost belongings.

"I'm sure it's haunted," said John.

"Crab apples!" snorted Maggie, and she tugged his hair then rushed across the garden that once had been a graveyard, and bobbed down the steps.

John smiled and wandered after his sister. He paused among the rhubarb to watch bluebottles skidding on the warm leaves, then went under the sunken archway, through the house's cool hall, and up two brass steps.

On the top step Maggie huddled at a little churchy door. "You knock," she whispered, so John knocked, and held his breath.

"Come in, children. In, in, in, in!"

Sunlight, flooding through a vast pointed window, made a dazzling blob of Great-grandfather Harris's armchair.

His delicate voice spilled over wonderful furniture, rolled around rows of books, floated over stuffed animals and brass instruments, and sank eventually into layers of precious rugs.

John's eyes slid at Maggie and he grinned with excitement.

Strange things happened in this room with its ceiling full of church rafters, and the mysterious curtained gallery where Great-grandfather slept – if he ever slept – and the medical-looking machine that was a hoist for carrying the ancient man up and down with a sliding hiss and a juddering halt; and the fireplace roaring with logs.

"You like my box of tricks?" Great-grandfather Harris came from the dazzle beyond the armchair, and he was scarcely taller than the chair's back. He was short enough for the children to see the top of his head and the dab of paste that stuck his rust-coloured wig to his scalp.

Great-grandfather Harris was so old he was neither man nor woman, but a round smooth creature who no longer shaved his tissue-paper cheeks, and whose voice never descended to masculine richness, nor rose to feminine clarity.

12

He walked from the sunlight to the fire, beamed fatly, and opened his arms, welcoming the children to his box of tricks.

The room.

ANOTHER BOX OF TRICKS

"Welcome! Close the door!"

John turned away from Great-grandfather Harris to clutch the cool china handle.

The door sighed into its frame, and when John faced the room, the stuffed animals – the hedgehog at his hand, the fox nestling in the hearth, the snakes draped on antlers which were nailed to the gallery rail, the huddled mice, the great frog – why, even the unstuffed creatures – butterflies in glass domes, bugs in flat trays, the skeleton of a monkey that danced in frozen outrage high on a bookcase – for one awful, delicious moment – they *moved*.

"Ho! ho! ho! ho! ho!" breathed Great-grandfather Harris, and his little hands were white against his blue velvet jacket as he held his tummy.

"What is it!" cried Maggie. "Did you play a trick? Did I miss something?"

"I have a new trick, my darlings. Come close to the fire." His velvet arms fluttered, beckoning.

"You know I don't like to leave the warmth. You know also – " He beamed up at Maggie and she squirmed. He shone his smile on John, and John nodded, waiting. " – you know also that I seldom leave this room; that this amusing house which I built is only a ghostly memory for me.

"It is several winters since I was in the kitchen, and that was only because two crows crashed down this chimney, smothering the fire with soot, blackening my treasures with their soiled wings – and the kitchen was warm. But – " He moved cautiously into a vast chair, and perched with his feet swinging above the rugs, his fingers dangling at the fox's head.

"But. Today…" His voice rustled like butterflies' wings, and John knelt with Maggie at the fire, sweating with heat, chilled with excitement. "Today," whispered Great-grandfather Harris, "I went *outside!*"

John heard Maggie gasp, and he knew his own mouth was open. Great-grandfather Harris *outside!*

"But — " said John.

"I know!" squeaked Great-grandfather. "I know! But the sun stood so bright and the sky so blue, I do believe it was as hot as Timbuctoo! Did I tell you the story of my journey to Timbuctoo in 1893 – ?"

"But *outside!*" gasped Maggie.

"Yes! And haven't the plum trees grown!

The very rhubarb is as tall as I am! Of course, I can see it from the windows whenever I choose to open the curtains, but one forgets the reality... The world is beautiful..."

"The *trick*, Great-grandfather Harris!" shrieked Maggie quietly, and she reached out and almost touched his knee.

"I saw," said the ancient man, "the card table, and remembered my old friend Simon Welkin 1784, may his many sins be forgiven. R.I.P. That means, Rest in Peace, but we're not going to let him."

In the silence, after Great-grandfather's voice stopped so suddenly, the shadows ceased their endless creeping; the gallery curtains hung thick and still, and every creature, stuffed or unstuffed, turned its head to listen.

"What d'you mean?" gasped John. "You can't – "

"It's a joke!" cried Maggie hopefully.

"Some of my tricks are jokes," chuckled the old man. "Some of my jokes are tricks! But one or two of my funny little ideas..." His voice faded so that Maggie and John opened their mouths to hear better. "...are real."

John said, "We have to get washed before tea." For actually, he was sometimes nervous of Great-grandfather Harris, and escaping to ordinary things, like washing and eating, was like counting your fingers during an exciting film just to remind yourself it *was* a film.

"Oh, we have time!" said Great-grandfather. "Nellie knows you're here, all safe with me. It's only salad anyway, and won't get cold!"

Great-grandfather Harris wriggled his legs (very neat in tiny tweed trousers, with buttons instead of a zip); he wriggled until his feet touched the rugs, then he walked under the gallery where shadows were piled between two church windows, and – helped by the children – pulled a lion's skin aside.

Darkly, darkly sat a chest of wood with iron hinges that creaked exactly right as Maggie and John lifted the lid.

The old man's white hands floated inside, and pulled up a skull-cap, red as blood, with a golden tassel that matched Maggie's hair superbly; and a witch's hat for John, velvet like the night, sparkling with perfect constellations of stars.

Great-grandfather Harris swirled cloaks around their shoulders and John stared at Maggie, her brown limbs suddenly hidden by the surging blue cape, and she was no longer his sister but a beautiful elf conjured from the box of tricks.

Then she grinned, and she was just Maggie dressed up; and she tugged John's cloak straight, telling him he looked like a chicken leg ready for the oven, wrapped in silver foil.

But when they stopped giggling and turned their heads (just a smidgin) towards Great-grandfather Harris, that ancient man had disappeared.

SEVEN CANDLES TO LIGHT

Maggie's arms were bone-hard around John's neck as she squealed, and John gasped –

Great-grandfather Harris simply *couldn't* have walked out of sight! Why, they had only turned away for a moment...

"Watch it," said John, as Maggie's embrace tipped the witch's hat over his eyes, and when he looked again, there before him, among the bars of evening sunlight, was Great-grandfather, beaming proudly; then he vanished in a swish of darkness and his voice said, "Isn't it clever?"

He reappeared as if stepping through curtains. "It's simply the blackest cloak ever made. In this uncertain light, it's very difficult to see."

He pushed the hood down, and Maggie held John's hand as they followed Great-grandfather Harris's head – its wig somewhat squint, after the cloak's hood being dragged off it – back to the fire.

"Fetch the African stool, Maggie," said Great-grandfather Harris, and he waited as

Maggie staggered to him, carrying the stool by one of its twelve legs.

She dumped it by the hearth, and Great-grandfather sat on its circular top. "And if John would turn that handle..." Great-grandfather beamed like a cherub, and his fingers appeared from the invisible depths of his cloak, pointing.

John saw a black iron circle on the wall and it turned, cold in his hands, like a steering wheel. A fine chain unwound towards the ceiling. Something came down.

"It's a chandelier!" cried Maggie, and John wondered if Mummy and Dad knew what strange things happened every summer when he and Maggie were sent from London to get brown, and watch things grow.

He stopped turning as Great-grandfather's palm flashed up at him.

The chandelier, also black iron, and very churchy and dusty, hung just above the rugs.

Maggie hooked cobwebs from it with her finger, and Great-grandfather conjured a lighted taper which John guessed he had lit at the fire.

Maggie touched the taper to one of the chandelier's candles, letting the flame gnaw and hold. Then all seven candles rested crookedly in the chandelier, flames burning on their heads.

"Simon Welkin," intoned the strange creature who was their Great-grandfather. "We are waiting!" And the old man's delicate voice was full of authority, like a headmaster. "Simon Welkin! Come! We would converse with thee!"

John turned his glance from Great-grandfather's face, to Maggie. Her blue eyes were enormous, and her brown knuckles gleamed white among the folds of her cloak. She squeaked as one of the candles went out.

"Ah!" sighed Great-grandfather. "Welcome, my friend!"

Three more candles snuffed, leaving sudden columns of smoke.

"Welcome home! Welcome to summer time! We will walk again among the yew trees – "

Two more candles lost their flames, then the last one shrank until it was the merest glow barely clinging to the wick. It died, and the smell of wax was strong.

John's heart beat firmly. Would Simon Welkin actually appear? Was this just one of Great-grandfather's tricks? Or one of his little ideas that was real magic?

Maggie's red lips were open. Sweat crawled from under her cap. "Has it worked?" she gasped.

Before Great-grandfather could reply, something clicked at the far side of the room.

They all turned, cloaks shifting, yellow hair molten.

The door began to open.

STOPPING AT THE
COTTAGE GATE

A bell tinkled, and Maggie groaned. John sighed, and Great-grandfather slipped his cloak off, letting it vanish into the leaping shadows on the hearth.

"Food!" cried Aunt Nell, and she came in backwards, then towards them, jingling a silver bell, balancing a tray with Great-grandfather's meal of clear soup, a boiled duck egg, and toasted home-made bread with Marmite. "Really, Great-grandfather! You shouldn't sit on the stool! You could fall into the fire! Isn't it stifling!"

She placed the tray on a side table and dabbed her forehead with the back of her very large hand. "Salad's in the kitchen!" she boomed. "Take off these silly clothes! Wash!" she yelled as John and Maggie fled down the two brass steps out of Great-grandfather's room.

"Rotten Nellie!" cried Maggie as she washed her face. "She spoiled it! Always bashing into things with her big feet!"

John shared the towel with her and grinned. Maggie sounded as if she were describing herself – though her feet were as neat as the rest of her.

"But it may already have worked," said John. "Race you to the kitchen!"

"May have worked!" cried Maggie into her salad. "Might have worked! Clump! Clump! Nellie and her bell! 'Take off these silly clothes!' Into a magic spell as if she didn't know any better! How long has she looked after Great-grandfather? Hundreds of years! And still interrupts! Great donkey! Great Nellie!"

"She'll hear," laughed John. "Oh, she's coming!" And he crunched lettuce along with sliced-down hard-boiled duck egg, cackling at Maggie tearing her gammon, silently and savagely, with her teeth.

Aunt Nell slippered into the kitchen with Great-grandfather's tea tray swinging and the bell clucking in her fist.

"Good gammon?" she asked. "Best you ever tasted? Best you ever will taste?"

"Best we ever will taste, Aunt Nell," said Maggie so politely that John cackled again, "until the next slice."

"It's extremely good, thank you!" gasped John, as Aunt Nell's heavy gaze pressed down on him. "Much better than Harrods'!"

"I suppose," said Aunt Nell, "that Harrods is some sort of standard. When you've eaten that, there's rhubarb crumble and fresh cream." She leaned on the table, her large hands taking up enough space for two dinner plates. "REALLY FRESH!" she boomed, making a berry-red tomato leap from John's fork.

Then she slapped across the gravestones that made up the kitchen floor and worked very noisily at the distant sink; evening sunlight spread a halo around her thick body.

"That was close!" whispered John. "I'll bet you get more crumble than me!"

BANG! BANG! BANG!

John's tomato jerked again from his fork and escaped to the floor. It rolled along the join between two gravestones.

"Golly-cripes!" squeaked Maggie.

"It must be a giant at the front door!" shouted Aunt Nell.

"We'll go!" cried Maggie, and John followed her, half laughing at his aunt, wholly-curious about such a din. Why, it was like someone beating the door with a rock.

"Why not press the door bell!" he gasped as he skidded in the hall over church tiles, and helped Maggie drag the door wide.

"Somebody joking!" complained Maggie, and John agreed (without actually speaking) for the brick steps up to ground-level were quite empty of visitors, and the crimson flowers of Peter Pan stood very still between the bricks, and absolutely no one stood on the iron grid – which was a drain – that separated the steps from the house.

Maggie raced up the steps (with John behind her), and along the brick path. She hung over the graveyard wall –

"Nobody!"

John swept a glance into the rhubarb. He dodged among the fruit trees to the river bank to see if the door-thumper hid there! but –

No one.

He jogged beside the stream, then clambered round the ash tree close above the water –

He ran to the stone gateposts beside Maggie, and stared towards the village.

The road sat dusty and unused, and the empty cottage, with weeds in its chimneys, seemed to sag in the evening heat.

"There!" said John.

"Where? I don't see anything!"

"In the cottage. There's a face at the window! Upstairs! I'm sure there's a face!"

"Turnip!" cried Maggie. "It's a turnip on the window-sill!"

"I'm sure it moved."

"Turnips don't move! Unless it's that Dirk Tomshed! His head's a turnip! WE SEE YOU DIRK TOMSHED! Do you think it's him? It's not moving. Even *his* head's not as round as that. The sun's setting. The shadows of the trees are lying down to sleep."

"You're a poet, Maggie," smiled John.

A silvery tinkle turned them towards the house, and they ran, full of summer, to finish their salad.

"And was it a giant?" demanded Aunt Nell. She thumped down a glass dish bubbling with rhubarb crumble. The tabletop fizzed as the glass bottom scorched a circle in the wood.

"Yes, Aunt Nell," said Maggie. "It had drunk the river dry because it was so thirsty after eating the rhubarb in the garden, and it wanted to use the toilet – "

John shrieked, and Aunt Nell stared, then strode away, bottom jutting.

Maggie's lips fastened over a giggle. John cackled. He looked at Aunt Nell as she leaned on the sink, and he nodded to Maggie.

Aunt Nell was laughing privately.

"That was scrummy crumble!" cried Maggie.

"More cream?" Aunt Nell wobbled the large white jug under John's nose. "Perhaps John didn't enjoy my rhubarb crumble? Not up to Harrods' standard?"

"Easily up to Harrods' standard, Aunt Nell!" said John. "Far better! I could eat another whole plateful. May we go out again when we've finished? After we've said 'goodnight' to Great-grandfather Harris?"

"Mmmmm," said his aunt severely. She served more crumble, and left the kitchen carrying the tray.

She returned with Great-grandfather's dishes. "Great-grandfather asks you not to disturb him at the moment, because he is looking for something. Something important. But you may say 'goodnight' when you come in – "

"Oh, thanks, Aunt Nell – " said John.

"I shall ring the bell in half an hour – "

"We'll come straight back!" promised Maggie.

"Wait! Take the egg shells!"

John and Maggie stood, jiggling with impatience as Aunt Nell crushed Great-grandfather's egg shell and the salad egg shells into a paper bag. "Round the gooseberries with them!" she boomed. "Off you go!"

And they fled, up the brick steps to the garden, leaping over a stone face that lay cheek-down in the grass, startling the white duck, stopping at the gooseberry bushes in the shadow of the tower and scattering the egg shells among the roots.

"Present from Nellie!" yelled Maggie at the gooseberries.

"Shush!" said John. "She's at the kitchen window!" Maggie waved at the window and John waved, and they ran, pattering on the brick path, over the wall instead of between the gateposts, running on the dusty road.

Trotting among the shadows of the trees that leaned above the road.

Walking on the grassy verge.

Stopping at the cottage gate.

LOOKING IN A
STRANGE MIRROR

"I don't see a turnip," said John.

"It was that Dirk Tomshed. I told you."
Maggie lifted the gate and swung it back over
weeds.

"We can't get in," said John. "You know the
door's locked."

"If Dirk Tomshed can get in, I can get in."

"It's a bit dismal."

Maggie stopped and John waited beside her.

Red light from the sky scored the windows
like streaks of blood. The roof sagged more
than last year, with stone tiles shuffled into the
gutter. The roof's wooden bones stood white
with dead fungus.

"You can see the front door's still padlocked,"
said John. "We'll go round the side."

He strode through high grass, seeds itching
the sting on his knee, Maggie fingering his
back as they passed low cobwebby windows
and a door with curling paint.

"Somebody's pulled these hinges loose,"
said Maggie. "We can get in here." She gazed

up at the cottage. "If you really want," she whispered.

"If *I* want!" squawked John.

"Sssh!"

"Sssh?"

"I heard something!"

John listened. "I hear Aunt Nell's duck quacking. Why doesn't she give it a name?"

"Because she'll eat it at Christmas. Sssh! There's someone upstairs. Feet on the floorboards – golly-cripes!"

A cry, that made the hairs on John's arms stand on end, came from inside the cottage. Feet thundered down a staircase.

Maggie fled towards the gate.

The feet crashed down behind the door. A fat hand grasped the door beneath the top hinge.

Surely John recognized those fingers? He glanced after Maggie and glimpsed yellow hair up a tree – already! – at the roadside.

John grinned and stepped away from the door. The door leaned open, jamming at the bottom on weeds.

A large square head squeezed out, followed by a white T-shirt, then a large pale knee, a fat leg with a sock and a brown leather shoe.

John folded his arms.

The complete person burst free of the door. John saw that it was wearing the same blue shorts as last summer.

"Hello, Cowshed," he said, and Dirk

Tomshed stared as if he hadn't noticed John. Then he sucked in a huge breath, seemed to remember what he was running from, and lumbered through the gate and disappeared into the village.

John said, "Well."

He strolled to the door and peered under the loosened hinge. A staircase rose gloomily.

He listened.

He turned towards Maggie's tree, and though he couldn't see her, he waved.

He stepped carefully into the cottage.

A hole was worn in the linoleum where people had turned to use the stairs. The bannister was gritty under John's palm. It angled up steeply and stopped at a wooden head – like one of the stone heads in the garden, thought John. On the landing, a door stood open letting evening sunlight warm the walls.

The house felt empty, and John strode up boldly, *crunch!* on grit, *crunch! crunch!* across the landing, *crunch!* through the bright doorway! Why, there's nothing here to frighten a baby! *Crunch! crunch! crunch!* to the window. There's Maggie swinging down from the tree, looking as if she'd burgled somebody's safe. No turnip on the window-sill. Just a cigarette, half-smoked and a book of matches. Must have been Toolshed. A wardrobe, rather like the one Daddy paid four hundred pounds for in Kensington Church Street, only this one has no door. *Crunch!* to the wardrobe. Nobody in there. He! He! a pair of old man's trousers with the pockets pulled inside out. Oh, there's the wardrobe door flung down in the corner. It's like a coffin lid but with a mirror. Jolly dirty. I can hardly see… There I am. Give myself a wave. That's funny. I've stopped waving, but the mirror –

John put his hands on his knees and stared down.

The figure in the mirror was waving desperately.

TOMSHED, TOOLSHED, COWSHED!

"Oh," said John.

He heard Maggie among the weeds beside the cottage. "John?"

He said, "Oh-oh!" and clattered, skidding on grit, down the stairs, thump! onto the hole in the lino, leaping out the door, stopping at Maggie – staring at Maggie as if he hadn't noticed her, jerked a glance up at the cottage and rushed towards the gate –

He ran back, snatched Maggie's wrist, and fled, with her twisting and complaining at his side, her voice cracking among the trees by the road.

"John! Stop!"

He stopped, looking back.

The cottage sat by the grass verge, its windows black now, the roof sagging. God had stuck pink strips of cloud across the sky.

"John," said Maggie.

John didn't know what to say. His heart knocked as if it wanted out. He wondered – just for a moment – if Dirk Tomshed had played a trick with the mirror, but he knew that no one could.

Then he thought his eyes had been mistaken. Perhaps something on the crumbling ceiling, above the mirror, had waved in a breeze, making him think a hand was mixed up with his reflection. But there wasn't a breeze.

"John?"

"I don't know," said John.

"You don't know what?"

"It's time to go in."

Maggie gazed at the cottage. She shrugged slowly as if to make sure her body was still there. John understood. He wanted to pat a tree trunk just to feel how solid it was, but dusk was turning the trees into looming giants. Perhaps one of them had knocked on the church door, earlier. "Aunt Nell must have rung by now."

"I think she might," said Maggie. "I see you've put the turnip back on the window-sill."

"What?"

"After Dirk Tomshed ran away. You put – "

The light had changed again, and behind the upstairs window in the cottage, the turnip head stared out.

"You were playing," breathed Maggie hopefully.

"Oh. Yes," agreed John. "Same game as Toolshed. Batter down the stairs…" He stared very hard at the turnip.

Then he walked home with Maggie, talking

brightly. Past the ash tree. They strolled along the brick path padded with plants which John knew were pink, but now were pale dots floating in the shadow of the church.

As they descended the steps, the door opened, and they jumped. Aunt Nell towered down on them, bell poised.

"May we say 'goodnight' to Great-grandfather?" asked Maggie politely.

"You're just on time," said Aunt Nell suspiciously. "You'll be tired, I suppose?"

"A bit," said John.

"Go on." A hard kiss landed on John's brow. Maggie held her hair aside to receive hers. "Clean your teeth."

"Yes, Aunt Nell."

"Goodnight, Aunt Nell," said John.

They pattered across church tiles to the door of Great-grandfather's room, up the two brass steps, knock-knock, "In!" and in they crept, whuffing the door shut, gazing at the firelight, trying to see Great-grandfather Harris, for no lights were lit and curtains hung where the pointed window had let in the sun earlier in the evening.

Nothing moved.

Except the shadow of the monkey's skeleton which danced with silent fury on the bookcase. And the shadow of the fox on the hearth. And the shadow of the African stool with its twelve legs wobbling across the rugs like the legs of a large spider.

And Great-grandfather Harris, half-way between the floor and the balcony, floating slowly upwards.

STUMP AND FLAP

Maggie's breath struck John's cheek. Her fingernails dug into the tan on his arm.

"Keep calm," said John. *Hissssss!* said the snakes. "It's only Great-grandfather going up in the hoist." *Judder*, said the hoist stopping.

"Of course," gasped Maggie. "I knew all the time!"

"Goodnight, Great-grandfather Harris," said John.

"Goodnight! Goodnight, my pretty ones!"

"Goodnight, Great-grandfather!" cried Maggie. "Did you find what you were looking for?"

"Not quite! But I believe it's getting closer! Goodnight! I heard wonderful knocking on the door as I scraped my egg with a Marmite soldier! Was it someone interesting?"

"Just Dirk Tomshed," said John. "Playing the fool."

"Oh. Ho! Ho! If he's anything like his father, he isn't playing! Ho! A big lumbering boy. Walks as if his knees are tied together."

"That's right — " began Maggie.

"He must be middle-aged by now. Silly game for a middle-aged man."

"No, Great-grandfather," said Maggie. "He's fourteen."

"Fourteen?" Great-grandfather walked from the hoist to the gallery rail and his face was a pale blob looking down. "Another generation. *Tempus fugit*. Goodnight."

"Goodnight, Great-grandfather," said John and Maggie.

For a moment, they gazed again at the firelight. John looked for the chest where the cloaks and hats were kept, but the windows above the chest were curtained, and shadows slept beneath the window-sills.

John was in bed first.

A Chinese screen gave Maggie privacy. She cried, "Oh!" and John heard her fall.

"Now I'll have a bruise!" she moaned, and he smiled sleepily.

It was difficult not to fall in the tower bedroom, for the tower leaned out from the body of the house, and Great-grandfather had made the floor level, so if you looked at the walls, thinking they were straight, the floor felt like a slope, and you would stump and flap until you got the knack of it; but standing on one leg to step into pyjamas…

"Sit down," said John. "Then you'll manage."

"I'm ready!" gasped Maggie, and John, face stinging pleasantly with the day's sun, heard her tumble into bed.

"It wasn't much of a trick," said Maggie.

John remembered the turnip head staring from the cottage.

"I thought more would have happened," sighed Maggie sounding disappointed.

John frowned with his eyes shut. "Well *you* scarpered," he said, "when Cowshed flew down the stairs."

"What? I mean the candles going out – on the chandelier."

"Oh, that."

"I thought more would have happened."

"Maybe it did," murmured John.

"What did you say?"

"Go to sleep, Maggie."

John relaxed happily. He loved this strangest of all houses, with its window-sills in the flower beds and the stream wandering past the fruit trees, and the countryside in green and gold...

"Oh!" John woke. "Oh, Maggie." He pulled the sheet back over his legs. "I was asleep."

He spread himself flat, feeling heat rising off his skin. The sheet twitched away again.

"Maggie!" He leaned up on his elbow.

Twilight had slipped through the churchy windows. Maggie was a dark lump on the other bed. "Maggie?" John straightened the sheet.

Maggie didn't stir. She should have giggled at least. John knew, suddenly, that his sister was asleep.

Someone else had pulled away his sheet.

THE TICK TOCK OF THE RAILWAY CLOCK

John remembered Daddy's words: "The secret of not being afraid is to think about the other chap."

John tried, but his heart beat hard, for there wasn't another chap. He looked all round.

Between two of Great-grandfather's antique wardrobes stood a chair. John could see only the hairy-paw feet of the chair's front legs shining in the gloom. He fingered a sand-shoe from the floor and tossed it into the shadow that sat on the chair.

The sand-shoe struck the wooden seat. Maggie sighed.

John stared very hard at the Chinese screen. Twilight shone through patterned gaps in its wood. If someone was there, John would see his shape. But there was no one.

The tick of the L.N.E.R. clock, which Great-grandfather had found in a derelict railway station, filled John's ears. He tried not to hear it. He listened for a rustle of clothes.

Then he thought: We're up two turns of the

spiral staircase, and Aunt Nell is downstairs clanging about the kitchen. And nobody could come in the windows without a ladder, and without stepping on Maggie's bed. There simply can't be anyone… John rested his head back on the pillow.

QUACK! QUACK! Up he sat. "Oh!"

He gasped, "Golly-cripes!" in a whisper, and smiled at soft morning light peeping into corners of the room.

Quack! Quack! Quack!

Maggie groaned. "The sooner Nellie plucks that duck, the better! Ooooaaaow," she yawned. "Are you awake?"

"I'm half dressed!" John fastened his shorts.

Quack! Quack! Quack! Quack!

"What *is* the matter with that bird!" Maggie knelt up on her bed and levered open the church window. "Doesn't dawn smell fresh! Goodness! The poor thing's dashing around as if it's been stung! Come on!"

"Not in your pyjamas!"

"Oh, pants! There's nobody to see!"

"It's only five o'clock!" laughed John, as he plopped his head through a shirt. "Don't wake Nellie!"

But Maggie had hauled open the door and was padding barefoot down the stairs.

John stuffed his toes into one sand-shoe, found the second sand-shoe on the chair between the wardrobes, hopped into it, darted down the curve of the iron stairs, hesitated on the bottom step, because there were three ways to go, heard a door-catch click, and dashed along a stone floor to one of the church's back doors.

The morning was grey, for the sun had really not got out of bed, so it was rather like running at dusk, except there were no flies, and birds were chorusing.

Maggie, in her pyjamas, was a blue-striped ghost dashing about the lawn. "The grass is wet! Ooh! It's cold!"

"You're scaring the duck!" cried John, for the duck was rushing here and there among the yew trees, wings flapping, beak threatening.

"It's chasing something!"

"There's nothing to chase!" John tried to blink away the gloom of early morning.

"It's quackers!" cried Maggie. "He! He! He! He! He!"

"Look at this."

Maggie wheeled towards him, and stopped. She said, "Oh."

In the shelter of a stone head, yolk and egg white oozed from a shell.

"It's newly broken," said John. "And look at the duck."

The duck went squawking around the corner of the church, fury in its stretched neck and beating wings.

John ran after it, but the duck came waddling

towards him, muttering, and settled in the grass, looking as severe as Aunt Nell.

"Race you round the church!" said John suddenly. Maggie frowned at him. "You go that way! I'll go past the rhubarb! First back here wins! Go!"

He ran quietly.

He ran close to the stream, peering.

He dashed to the graveyard wall and looked along the road. Maggie passed him, flying, like a yellow nun in the grey light. The deserted cottage was the colour of a pencil drawing. There was someone hurrying away from John, towards it. No there wasn't. Funny how dim light plays tricks. He couldn't make out if the turnip still watched from the upstairs window.

He found Maggie sitting on the grass, discussing motherhood with the duck. "I win!" she cried at John.

"I didn't see anyone."

"You were supposed to be racing!"

"Someone," said John, "broke the egg."

"The duck broke the egg."

"It was chasing something. And last night—"

"Well, I win anyway. Even if you weren't trying. What about last night?"

"Nothing. Couldn't sleep, at first. What'll we do until breakfast?"

"I'm going to dress," said Maggie, standing up and peeling her pyjama seat off her skin. "My botty's wet."

THE VOICE OF DOOM!

They idled through a couple of hours, swinging on a tyre which Aunt Nell had hung for them years before, on the fleshy red arm of a yew.

They watched mist rising from the stream, and rabbits bob-tailing on the path where John had found the dock. The sun shrank the shadow of the church, and tried to toast the ground for breakfast.

Then Aunt Nell was rattling around the kitchen and they burst in on her and set the table, chattering, preparing Great-grandfather Harris's tray; choosing duck eggs from the box delivered by the butcher's van on Thursdays; pausing, though, when Aunt Nell glanced at the four eggs they put into her hands.

"What's wrong?" asked Maggie.

Aunt Nell returned one egg to Maggie's palm.

"Great-grandfather does not eat the butcher's eggs," announced Aunt Nell. "As you know!"

"Of course we know, Aunt Nell, but the duck's duck egg is broken. On the grass."

Aunt Nell's back straightened, taking her nose high enough to stare down it.

"It's broken," squeaked Maggie.

"It is," said John.

"And HOW!" boomed their aunt, "DID IT BREAK?"

"We don't know," said John.

"SOMEONE BROKE IT!"

"We didn't see anyone," whispered Maggie.

"I SEE TWO SOMEONES!" Aunt Nell took the fourth egg from Maggie's palm. "*Great-grandfather will be informed!*"

John laid his hand on Maggie's arm. "We didn't break it, Aunt Nell."

Aunt Nell presented her back. Her head rose proudly. Maggie stepped away, and pointed at her aunt's skirt. Aunt Nell's bottom jutted.

"We didn't break it," said John, through a laugh.

The eggs descended into a pan of boiling water.

"The duck woke us," pleaded Maggie, "and we ran down to see what was wrong. I think it was that Dirk Tomshed."

"Sit! at the table."

They sat.

They waited.

Aunt Nell served their eggs then swept away with Great-grandfather's tray, the silver bell piercing the house.

"We're getting the blame," said Maggie.

"You made me laugh," said John.

"Rotten Nellie."

"This feels like a Grand Silence." John reached for the toast made of Aunt Nell's home-made bread. He spread, munched, crunched, enjoyed the extra-egginess of the duck egg.

Heavy slippers sounded beyond the kitchen. The tray bonged – against Aunt Nell's leg – thought John.

In she came, *bong*, on her leg. Served her own egg, sat, scratched butter onto toast, cut off her egg's head, poured tea, ate, drank, sat very straight. Said – in a voice of doom – "*When you have eaten, Great-grandfather will speak to you in his room.*"

DOOM'S VOICE

"Oh!" breathed Maggie over her glass of milk.

Her glance slid at John, and he laid his slice of toast on his plate. "I don't think I can eat any more, thank you, Aunt Nell."

"Not surprised." Egg wobbled on Aunt Nell's spoon. "Go and see him. Both of you. Go, go."

With looks and sighs, John led Maggie up the brass steps to tap on Great-grandfather's door, and they went in at the ancient man's call.

The fire blazed. The curtains shut in shadows. It was hard to think that outside the sun was glaring into every corner of the countryside.

"Good morning, Great-grandfather Harris," whispered Maggie.

"Good morning, Great-grandfather," said John.

Great-grandfather – perched on a dining chair with a cushion under his tweed trousers, and his feet on the rungs like a naughty boy – was reaching across his table.

He said, "Ah."

Maggie darted to put the marmalade pot within Great-grandfather's reach.

"Thank you, Maggie, and good morning. Good morning, John. It's very nice to see you again."

He dipped his knife into the pot. "Don't tell Nellie that I never use her spoon for the marmalade," said Great-grandfather. "It's so tiny it takes twenty journeys to fetch enough to cover my toast! Ho! Ho!"

He eased his wrists out of his blue velvet cuffs and began spreading. "And what are your plans for today? Sun's shining, so Nellie tells me. You're looking very sombre – "

"We're sorry about your egg, Great-grandfather!" burst out Maggie.

"That's very kind, Maggie, but there's no need. I'm sure the duck doesn't miss it, and it was delicious as usual." He leaned towards the children and whispered. "Sometimes Nellie slips me a butcher's egg, but I always know." He winked over his teacup.

Maggie's cheeks bunched into a smile and she looked at John. Aunt Nell hadn't mentioned the broken egg!

John's shoulders relaxed. If there was one person in the world he didn't want to upset, it was Great-grandfather Harris.

He remembered that Great-grandfather had asked about their plans.

"We're going to see Dirk Tomshed." John felt Maggie's stare. "He was in the ruined cottage. I think he was trying to frighten us. He didn't succeed." Maggie's hair dipped like gold flowing as she bent her head. "I thought I'd have a talk with him."

"Quite."

Great-grandfather sighed, and his glance blinked towards John. "Quite!" he said brightly.

"Are you all right, Great-grandfather?" asked John, for Great-grandfather's fingers drummed chubbily on his table mat. "Is something the matter, Great-grandfather?"

"What? Oh, no, no, no, no, no…"

Great-grandfather's fingers tapped the silver bell. He raised his eyebrows at no one in particular. He said again, "No… Well, yes, John, since you ask. Pull the table back, my darlings. Thank you. Let me lean on your shoulders… Chairs never used to be so high. Since you ask…"

He walked to the fire and stared into the roaring blaze. A bit of egg shell clung in the turn-up of his trousers. John saw Maggie staring at it, but neither of them dared lift it out – or even mention it – while Great-grandfather was thinking.

Great-grandfather's silence went on.

The fire snarled at his legs but he paid no heed.

Electric lamps gazed onto the precious rugs.

The monkey's skeleton grinned down at Great-grandfather's wig. The old gentleman's fingers gathered at his back and wiggled like uncooked sausages.

"You will recall," he said, "my little game with Simon Welkin."

Great-grandfather backed towards the armchair and Maggie rushed to help.

"I think – thank you Maggie – that – quite inadvertently – we have done him some mischief. Ring the bell, please, John. And it really isn't clever to do mischief to Simon Welkin. Something bad," nodded Great-grandfather to the flames, "is sure to come of it."

"But, Great-grandfather," said John, as calmly as if he were ordering ice-cream in a café, "surely Simon Welkin is dead? How – ?"

"Of course he's dead, my dears. Don't we have his gravestone between the rhubarb and the stream? Aren't his initials carved on the heads that lie about the garden – ?"

"Simon Welkin made the heads?"

"Exactly. He was a stone mason of this parish – "

"But if he's dead, Great-grandfather," insisted John, "how can we have done him any harm?"

"Yes! Great-grandfather!" squealed Maggie.

"Why – " Great-grandfather Harris slid back into the armchair until the soles of his slippers caught the firelight. " – you can't have forgotten that we called Simon Welkin from under his card table, and that he sucked the flames off the candles?"

The ancient man chuckled suddenly, so that his tummy shook inside its blue velvet jacket.

"I remember the day he made a bet with Dan Tomshed. No, John, you don't know this Tomshed. He lived long ago when I was a young man. Tomsheds, my darlings, have farmed here for generations. Well, Dan Tomshed was a bull – strong but thick-headed! A good farmer though, with a fine herd of cattle. Trouble was," Great-grandfather sighed, "no one would work for him. He was a bad-tempered bull. So he had to clean his byre himself, and Simon Welkin made a bet that *he* could clean Tomshed's byre in no more than one hour by the church sundial.

"Simon teased Tomshed, so that the bet got bigger and bigger until folk began to think either Simon had lost his reason – for it was a huge byre – or Tomshed would lose his farm.

"Tomshed lost his farm." Great-grandfather Harris leaned towards John and Maggie (who were now sitting on the precious rugs not too close to the fire).

"Simon used to read the classics. He said they gave him ideas. Have you heard of Hercules and the cleansing of the Aegean Stables? Where Hercules turned a river, to wash the stables clean? Simon Welkin got his apprentices to load eight great stones onto a cart. Up past the five-bar gate they went, and dumped the stones in the water."

"But – "

"But how did he know the stream would go through Tomshed's byre? Because he planned it. He had seen the lie of the land, and how with a bit of night-time digging, the stream would run exactly through the byre. And that's what gave him the idea of making the bet with Tomshed. Tomshed had no chance, for Simon Welkin never took a chance. He *knew* the stream would wash the byre!"

"But Great-grandfather!" John wriggled. Would Great-grandfather *ever* answer his question! "If he's dead – "

"That's not the end of the story!" breathed the old gentleman. "Ah, Nellie with her tray."

"Oh," said Maggie.

"Hello, Aunt Nell," said John. He had quite forgotten that Great-grandfather Harris was supposed to be giving him and Maggie a row.

Aunt Nell strode to Great-grandfather's table and cleared the dishes. The bell tinkled timidly amid her silence. She stood with the tray, waiting.

"Goodbye, Great-grandfather," sighed John. Maggie stood up. "Goodbye, Great-grandfather Harris."

As they left the box of tricks – with Aunt Nell heavy behind them in her slippers – something dropped from the balcony, and found its way onto Maggie's turned-up palm.

GREAT-GRANDFATHER'S TURN-UP

They strode in silence through the church. John looked at Maggie's fist, clenched in front of her. He had glimpsed something pale flickering down in the shadow of a pillar, and Maggie's hand cupping to meet it.

Aunt Nell's tread bustled them into the kitchen.

She dumped down the tray.

"Did Great-grandfather – " demanded Aunt Nell, a quiver in her voice, " – speak to you about THE EGG!"

John opened his mouth –

"Yes!" said Maggie. "He said quite a lot about the egg."

John shut his mouth. That was true. Great-grandfather *had* said a lot about the egg. And Aunt Nell – he realized, with a little scowl – had, after all, told Great-grandfather about the egg being broken.

He knew what was coming.

"I think I deserve recompense," whispered Aunt Nell. The quiver in her voice trembled her head. "Since *you* have been here – "

What *was* she going to get them to do? Last year it had been scrubbing the kitchen floor which she claimed still had soot in the gravestones from the previous winter when the crows had crashed around Great-grandfather's room, and he had walked the soot through the house.

"Since you have been here," quavered Aunt Nell, "I have been EXTREMELY BUSY baking rhubarb crumble, preparing hams, jams and lamb. Washing dishes, pulling plums – which you will have this evening! Buying chocolate…"

"We'd like to help, Aunt Nell," said Maggie solemnly.

Aunt Nell stared at Maggie, then swept Great-grandfather's tray away, down the length of the kitchen, to the sink.

"The lawn needs to be cut."

"So that's why she's in the huff!" whispered Maggie. "It's to get us to mow the lawn! She knows perfectly well we'd've owned up if we'd broken her mouldy egg!"

"The lawn is outside." Aunt Nell's voice came back to them off the window panes. "Where it has always been."

"Where it has always been!" sniped Maggie.

"I haven't heard the door closing."

"I haven't heard the — "

John cackled and rushed Maggie from the kitchen.

He wanted to know what Great-grandfather had magicked into Maggie's hand. She seemed to have forgotten.

"It will take both of us to haul that lawn-mower!" yelped Maggie.

"Maggie!" said John. "What fell into your hand?"

"Oh!"

They stood in a passage that led to a back door. Portraits in gold frames stared from both walls.

Maggie opened her hand and laughed.

John grinned. "Great-grandfather," he said. "He knew all along that Aunt Nell had sent us in for a row. This is to tell us he didn't mind about the egg."

On Maggie's palm was the piece of shell from the turn-up of Great-grandfather's trousers.

EATING THE THIRD PLUM

The lawn was as big or as small as you wanted. Among the yew trees, grass stood stiff and tall in the morning heat, and nobody would call *that* lawn. At least, not until it was cut. And if you didn't cut it, it stayed just grass-among-the-yews.

And sometimes the fruit trees grew out of *lawn*, or out of grassy ground, depending on whether anyone felt like pushing the mower over it.

Lawn*ish* places lay between flower beds, but stones fallen from the tower, or gravestones no one had bothered to move, slept in the grass, preventing any straightforward mowing.

So it was sometimes better to say that just *this* small grassy space will be lawn today, and perhaps – if we're enjoying the exercise, or it doesn't rain – between the rhubarb and the crab apples *also* will be lawn – though if the duck is dozing there, well! it wouldn't do to disturb it. Especially since it was to be eaten at Christmas.

However, an aunt's angry eye at the kitchen

window makes one small patch of cut grass seem not enough, so perhaps under the plum trees needs to be cut, and – you never know – a plum or two might fall, just when children are getting hot and thirsty.

John and Maggie had talked about meanie aunts, and decent great-grandfathers during the mowing, and they had stopped to rescue three plums from the blades by sitting at the stream and eating them, then – in the middle of a really interesting moan from Maggie about aunts who blackmail young relatives into slavery – John sat up very straight.

He remembered the paintings in the passage to the back door.

He remembered the faces of men and women in old-fashioned clothes.

He remembered one face…

"John! Where are you going!"

"Come on!" said John.

He ran among the gardens, darted down the steep path to the back door, and stood before one painting. "Who does that remind you of?"

"Nobody!" sighed Maggie.

"Oh, do think! Do look and think! Imagine he's not wearing that hat! Hasn't he got a big round head? Fat cheeks?"

"Nobody."

"*What* does it remind you of?"

"He! He! A turnip! Like on the window-sill in the ruined cottage! Another turnip head!"

John walked Maggie back to the lawn-mower and sat with her, staring into the stream while she chattered. Boulders draped with dry plants sat out of the water.

"Maggie," said John. "I must tell you."

"What? Who's going to eat the last plum?"

"You eat it. Maggie, there wasn't any turnip in the cottage."

"Yes, there was. We saw it when we looked back from the road."

"It wasn't in the room."

"Of course it was."

"Maggie." John waited while Maggie spat the plum stone into the stream.

"What? Good plums! Plums for tea! Nellie said so! I'm glad she's a great cook!"

"Maggie, there really wasn't a turnip."

Maggie's blue eyes steadied on John. "You're trying to frighten me."

"I didn't tell you before, because I knew you'd be scared. But I've got to tell you. Then we must talk to Great-grandfather."

"But if it wasn't a turnip… " Maggie ducked her face, putting her hair between herself and John.

"Maggie. I think it was Simon Welkin."

SOMETHING IN THE STREAM

"You don't!" cried Maggie. "You don't! You don't! You want to scare me because you're fed up mowing the lawn! Take that!" And a slap landed on John's head.

John rubbed his scalp.

Maggie clutched her knees, rocking.

"You know I wouldn't, Maggie." John gazed at the rocks in the stream. One stuck up among river plants, looking rather square.

"The painting has Simon Welkin's name under it – "

"Don't care!"

"It's not just that. There's a mirror in the cottage. You remember I ran down the stairs? And Dirk Tomshed ran down the stairs?"

Maggie stared at John through her hair. "It was a game."

"There was someone in the mirror," said John quietly, "waving at me."

"Hmph!"

"I couldn't see very well because the room was gloomy and the mirror was very dirty, but

60

it could have been someone in old-fashioned clothes. With a turnipy head."

Maggie, embracing her knees, rocked.

Water bubbled around the square stone.

John rose, and stepped among boulders. He patted the stone and saw that water and plants covered most of it, and that only the end was square. It was almost as tall as John, though, of course, it was lying down.

"Look at this, Maggie."

"Hmph!"

"I think it's a sundial!" Water cooled his fingers as he pulled plants aside. "It must have been here for years. There's no metal bit on top."

"You're saying that Simon Welkin is in a mirror! *And* at the cottage window!"

John nearly said, "*And* hammering on the church door like a giant. *And* in our bedroom, pulling my sheet away. *And* in the garden, being chased by the duck." But he didn't.

Instead, he said, "Come and help!"

Maggie splashed beside him, four hands together gripping the stone top. "Mind your toes!" said John. "Heave!"

But the sundial only grated.

"Oh! Here's Nellie! Jump off the roof, Nellie!" whispered Maggie.

Aunt Nell strode across the lawn, through the orchard, sturdy, elbows out, standing beside the lazy mower –

"Oh," sighed John.

But Aunt Nell ignored the mower and said, "Finding treasure? Pirate's chest? Giant's wooden leg? Haw! Haw!"

"I think it's a sundial," said John.

"It's terribly heavy, Aunt Nell."

"Oh, is it! We'll see about that!"

Through the boulders she strode – John and Maggie paddled backwards out of the way – grasp! "Hup!" and hup came the sundial, with water draining from the plants –

"It wouldn't dare just lie there!" whispered Maggie.

Aunt Nell rested, the dial leaning into her hands. "Fetch a rope!" she panted. "In the gardening room!"

They returned in a minute and bound the rope round the square end still in the water, and they *hupped*, stepping cautiously onto the grass, down! with the square end! Aunt Nell raising her end, steadying the ancient stone with its dial to the sun.

"THERE!" boomed Aunt Nell. "Thought it was heavy!?"

John wondered if she meant *they* had dared think it was heavy, or the sundial had dared think it was heavy. He smiled. And Maggie smiled. And Aunt Nell smiled.

"Enough grass-cutting for one day – "

"Thank you, Aunt Nell!" simpered Maggie.

"You can do more tomorrow... This *is* a

find! Great-grandfather will be interested! Come along! It won't fall over!" She paused to peer at the sundial through its green jacket of plants. "Very handsome, I would say! Come along! This sun is hot! Great-grandfather should be *outside!*"

WHAT WILL HE DO TO US?

"Do you think I dare?" Great-grandfather blinked at his overcoat in Aunt Nell's grasp.

"Of course, Great-grandfather!" cried Maggie.

"Yes, Great-grandfather," said John.

Why, they had never *seen* Great-grandfather Harris outside!

"Now, Nellie, is it really warm enough? Yesterday – "

"It's as hot as yesterday." Aunt Nell held the coat ready to be filled by Great-grandfather's arms.

"We've found a sundial!" squealed Maggie.

"A sundial? Well! I mentioned a sundial only this morning! Hold the coat higher, Nellie. I'm not a child. Where's my Rupert scarf? Thank you. Gloves. Hat. Maggie, turn the brim up for me, there's a good girl. Now I can see."

"You do look funny, Great-grandfather."

"I know," said Great-grandfather. "You've forgotten my shoes, Nellie. Oh, you haven't. Just let me lean on you, children, while your aunt ties my laces. A double knot, please Nell. Thank you. Oh. Outside twice in two days! How heavy all these clothes are! Stay on either side of me, children. I'm ready, Nell. Open the door!"

They went through the passage where the portraits stared from both walls.

John paused at Simon Welkin, and waited while Great-grandfather looked at the portrait and nodded.

Then they pushed Great-grandfather up the steep path from the door, past the yew trees, into the shadow under the tower, then over the lawn, the old gentleman breathing deeply every step and saying, "Aaah!"

He blinked up from under his hat, at the tower, until he staggered, laughing. John and Maggie steadied him. "You'd think the tower was falling," he said, "when you stare at the sky. Now – "

The children led him past the lawn-mower and pointed at the sundial. Aunt Nell patted the sundial as if she had made it herself.

"I'd like to sit down," said Great-grandfather Harris, and Maggie grabbed the grass-bin from the lawn-mower and stood it on end, then all three balanced the old gentleman on the other end.

Aunt Nell stood beside Great-grandfather,

her hand on his shoulder, while John and Maggie tugged the plants from the sundial.

"I told the children that Simon Welkin means mischief," said Great-grandfather.

"Really," said Aunt Nell, as if she knew all about Simon Welkin.

"What will he do to us, Great-grandfather?" lisped Maggie.

"The trouble was, my dears, that Nell came in ringing her bell just as the candles puffed out on the chandelier. SOUND is an important tool in magic. Remember how I commanded Simon Welkin to appear, with such authority? Well, Nell's bell broke the spell, and poor old Simon is sort of still here."

"Sort of where, Great-grandfather?" asked John.

"Mm. If the spell had been completed, Simon Welkin would have appeared, we'd have had such an interesting chat about the old days, then he'd have gone away again. But with only half the spell, he won't go until he's strong enough to finish his mischief."

Maggie stopped tugging at the sundial's green jacket. She shrank against John. "What will he do to us, Great-grandfather?"

"To us? Why, nothing, Maggie! I'm his old friend! But I *am* worried about what he'll do to the Tomsheds."

TOMSHED THROWS A GRAVESTONE

"We really don't understand," said John, and he sat on the grass, pulling Maggie down with him. They waited to be told.

"I was telling you about Simon's bet with Dan Tomshed," said Great-grandfather. "Well, from the sniggering in the village, and knowing the cunning nature of Simon Welkin, Tomshed soon guessed that he had been cheated out of his farm. He grew very angry.

"He sat in the public house, getting angrier.

"It rained. It rained so hard that puddles were full of bubbles. Of course, Simon Welkin had made his apprentices remove his stones from the stream, so the water ran again in its old course. But because of the rain, there was a lot more of it – water in the stream, I mean.

"Now, I told you that Tomshed was a bull, and not very bright – "

Nodding, from John and Maggie.

" – but he knew a good idea when he saw it. So as he sat in the public house watching the rain battering the puddles, he realized that he could do what Simon Welkin had done."

Great-grandfather's head turned in the shade of its hat and nodded at the church.

"The church," breathed Great-grandfather, "was Simon Welkin's pride and joy, because, not only had he carved all the gravestones for three generations, but he had added so much in the way of decoration to the church building. Well, one *extremely* wet evening…"

The children settled deeper into the grass, and Aunt Nell bent her head.

"…Tomshed rose from his ale and went striding into the night.

"Only one person paid any attention." Great-grandfather patted himself carefully on the chest, and John gaped.

"I could see he was up to something. I was afraid he would lay hands on Simon. So I followed him.

"Oh, it was a most fearsome night! The wind blew. The rain poured. The moon peeped now and then from behind the clouds, so I only glimpsed Tomshed, following him mainly by the thumping of his feet and the rage growling in his throat."

Great-grandfather leaned towards John and Maggie so that Aunt Nell had to save him from falling off the grass-bin.

"He tramped past Simon Welkin's cottage, and headed here! to the graveyard. I thought he was going to break the church windows!

No! What did he attack? Why, *that!*"

Great-grandfather pointed. "The sundial! He had lost the bet by an hour measured on that dial! And he tore it from the ground! My! My! I'm not all that big," said Great-grandfather as if no one had noticed, "and I wasn't a lot bigger then – and to see this man lift all that stone! carry it to the stream with the moon gleaming on his wet shoulders – and hurl all that weight into the water! If there hadn't been so much water the sundial would have smashed. The water was like a cushion, you see. But did Tomshed stop there? He did not.

"He lifted the nearest gravestone. I thought it would follow the sundial. But no! No! Do you know what he did? He stood. Looking. With the moon peering fearfully, and rain running down the huge stone in his arms. He walked along the bank, choosing just the right place – I remember he stopped beside a young ash tree – and he heaved the stone into the stream. Then he lifted another and flung it after the first. And another. And – "

" – another!" squeaked Maggie.

"Mmm!" agreed Great-grandfather. "Then he stepped back. I watched from the graveyard gate.

"A monster of water came snarling over the river bank, and I realized what Tomshed had done. Why, he'd blocked the stream with gravestones, so that the water rushed out to gobble up the church!"

THE SINKING OF
THE CHURCH

"Oh!" gasped Maggie.

"Golly-cripes!" whispered John.

Aunt Nell said nothing, but patted Great-grandfather's coat collar close around his scarf.

"Well, I ran," said Great-grandfather. "To fetch Simon Welkin. His cottage was close by. In fact – " Grandfather's fist came up and released a finger. " – I do believe…"

"The ruined cottage!" said John.

"So it is. So it is. And is that an ash tree? Anyway. I raised the alarm. Simon came. The men from the public house came. But no one could do anything. The graveyard was a lake. Inside the church the pews were under water. It was only then that people realized the church was built in a saucer of ground.

"So we lifted the gravestones from the stream. Tomshed helped. He knew he was in the wrong. But it was too late. The rain fell as if God was emptying his bathtub.

"The water had no chance of draining away.

"Simon Welkin raged. But he could do

nothing to save his church, and he could do nothing to Tomshed because people were beginning to see that Simon was more wrong than Tomshed.

"Weeks went by. The lake sat flat with the church sticking out of it. Then one terrible day…"

Maggie shivered as if the sun had lost its heat.

"…the church began to sink."

"Ah," said John.

"The tower leaned."

"Of course!" whispered Maggie.

"Stones fell from the tower, splashing down to the sunken graveyard. And when Simon Welkin saw this, he began carving his finest piece of white marble."

"I know!" said John.

"You know what?" cried Maggie.

"I know what he made from the marble!"

"Do you, now?" said Great-grandfather Harris.

"Tell me! Tell me!"

"He made the card table!" said John. "He made his own gravestone! Am I right, Great-grandfather?"

"Yes," said Great-grandfather sadly. "You are right, John. And when he was finished carving – he died.

"His church was ruined, you see, and the gravestones he had carved so lovingly were broken by Tomshed when he crashed them one on top of the other into the river. And it seemed to me – " Great-grandfather gazed at John and Maggie. He looked fondly up at Aunt Nell.

" – it seemed to me that Simon Welkin, yesterday evening, was knocking on our door."

"Oh, no!" gasped Maggie.

"I think so too," said John firmly.

"There's no other knock, like a knock from beyond the grave," said Great-grandfather. "Yes, John?" he asked, for John's hand had raised itself as if he were in class.

John glanced at Maggie. "Sorry, Maggie. Don't be scared." He faced Great-grandfather. "I think Simon Welkin broke your egg – "

"Humph!" from Aunt Nell.

"I think Maggie and I both saw him at the cottage window. We thought he was a turnip. And I saw him in a mirror inside the cottage."

"Of course!" breathed Great-grandfather. "Letting you see him through glass is the only way for a ghost who is only half here. He wanted help."

"And," said John, "he pulled the sheet off my bed."

"Then – " Great-grandfather tidied the flap of his coat over his knees. " – he is getting stronger. Pulling off your sheet, John, and breaking the egg takes a lot of energy for a ghost. Much more than appearing in a mirror or at a window. And once he's strong enough –"

Great-grandfather's head shook solemnly under his hat. " – he will want his revenge. That's why I'm anxious about the Tomsheds."

PART TWO

TEENSY WEENSIES

Oh! but a summer day lies hot and slow! And hot it certainly was. And slow it was for John and Maggie, waiting for something to happen.

It was so hot! they rinsed their faces in the stream. It was so slow that Maggie ran into the kitchen and returned to John, saying, "Half past ten just!" Then ages later, she dashed again, and trailed back saying, "Five to eleven, golly-cripes."

So they paddled under the ash tree, finding bits of broken gravestone thrown by Tomshed. Then Maggie suggested they should count the stone heads lying around the church, but they nearly quarrelled about *that* because Maggie insisted she had won because she said, "Fourteen," when John found only nine.

But John pointed out Simon Welkin's initials cut on one head and Maggie forgot about winning. Seeing SW cut into the stone made Simon Welkin suddenly more real. Both children gazed around the garden – though, honestly, neither of them felt any ghostly presence.

Which was disappointing.

And a relief.

The afternoon dragged as if someone had tied gravestones round its ankles. The children dozed under a yew tree, their rubber tyre dangling in the heat. The yew tree's shadow covered them like a spider's web, keeping off the sun's claws.

Then after tea (with yumptious plum pudding), John borrowed a book from Great-grandfather and worked at cutting and bending a metal triangle and a metal square from a rusty biscuit-tin which he dug out of the gardening room. Then, with careful reference to the book, he marked lines and numbers on the square and drew Simon-Welkin faces on the triangle.

Maggie, of course, did something equally useful: she talked to the duck; she chewed grass, with her legs waving (and getting very brown indeed); she stared up at the church tower until it seemed to be falling; she flattered Aunt Nell into showing her how to make real lemonade and gave John a small glassful and drank a large glassful herself.

"What are you making?" she managed to ask.

"Sundial," said John, and that was the end of that conversation.

The only teensy weensy odd thing that happened – and, really, nobody paid any attention to it – was when dusk was crowding the tower bedroom and John and Maggie (clean and cool after baths) were hopping about on the unsloped floor trying to get into pyjamas.

The door crashed open and Aunt Nell came in to thud a kiss on each forehead. Then she went out, and John stood blinking, because he had not heard Aunt Nell coming up the iron stairs, nor could he hear her going down.

Suddenly (John wasn't quite sure why) he ran and opened the door and called, "Goodnight, Aunt Nell!"

Aunt Nell's slippers still struck silent on the steps, but she looked up through the twists of the iron bannister and sent John another "Goodnight!"

The duck wakened John and Maggie at a more human hour than yesterday, and breakfast was jolly because Great-grandfather's egg came from the duck and not from the butcher.

John forgot about Aunt Nell's slippers and the only teensy weensy odd thing that happened – and, really, nobody paid any attention to it – was Aunt Nell frowning at her bell and shaking it close to her ear; it sounded a bit muffled to John, and Maggie didn't notice because she was nagging for a picnic lunch.

John's plan for the morning – after finishing mowing between the fruit trees – was to fix the tin square and triangle to the sundial, then move the whole thing to the sunniest place in the garden.

Using a tube of glue and screws, John attached the bits of tin. Then with the rope, and a scrap of carpet as a sledge (once the glue was dry) and Maggie pulling beside him, he hauled the sundial past the gooseberry bushes, and stood it well outside the tower's shade.

"It looks very grand," said Maggie. "Our very own sundial."

"We'll have to position it properly," said John.

"What do you mean?"

"Turn it so the shadow tells the correct time."

"Go on then."

"I have to know the time now."

"I'll look!" said Maggie, and dashed off.

John guessed it was quarter to twelve. He wrestled the stone until the triangle's shadow touched the quarter to twelve line on the tin square.

The sundial rocked as he leaned on it, so he pushed pebbles under until it stood firm.

He should have asked Aunt Nell for metal polish to take the rust off his tin.

Where was that Maggie? Drinking lemonade probably.

He turned towards the sunken door.

He turned, thinking of the sun doing its

work on the sundial, and for a moment glanced at the dazzling sky.

Blobs of lights spread between him and the church.

He blinked.

Something was running towards him.

Fast.

JUTTING SILENTLY

John stepped back.

His heel caught a tuft in the rough ground, and he sat bump! on the grass. The running thing came through the blobs of light –

" – JOHN!" bellowed Maggie. "ARE YOU DEAF?"

"Maggie!" gasped John.

"Nellie's been ringing the bell! She's mad!"

"I didn't hear – "

"And you ignored *me!* Screaming, *Grub's ready! Picnic's ready!* Now she's in a double huff – !"

"Oh," groaned John.

"Get up! What are you doing down there, anyway?"

"I couldn't see you for the sun. And you were so quiet – "

"Quiet!? My lungs were inside out!"

John – walking quickly with Maggie across the lawn – stared at her.

"You were really shouting? From the

doorway?" He stopped, and looked at the doorway. He looked back at the sundial. "Maggie." He stretched as if measuring the distance between the doorway and the sundial. "It's only a couple of cricket pitch lengths. "You couldn't have been screaming – "

"Of course I was screaming! *Grub's ready! Picnic's – !*"

"All right," laughed John.

They pattered down the brick steps, out of the dazzle of sunlight, blinking into the kitchen.

"Oh!" said John.

"Some picnic!" said Maggie, beaming at the table. "I helped. A bit. Wasn't I a help, Aunt Nell? Roast beef sandwiches – "

Aunt Nell, jutting silently, slapped down a tray. John and Maggie slid plates, two with the roast beef sandwiches, a long plate with sardines head-to-tail –

Another tray slapped down.

Tomatoes the size of strawberries; strawberries the size of tomatoes; home-made bread and newly-churned butter. Two jugs of lemonade; chocolate cake; Aunt Nell's biscuits that melted on your tongue –

"Is Great-grandfather coming?" asked John.

"Humph!"

"We didn't hear the bell. Really we didn't. And I didn't hear Maggie when she yelled, until she was really close – "

"Humph!"

John balanced more plates on the tray. "I think it's to do with Simon Welkin. Maggie's feet didn't make a whisper on the grass. It was as if she had burst out of a soundproof room... We'll need the tartan rug – "

"I'll get it!" said Maggie, and scarpered.

John went to his aunt and stared at her until she met his gaze. "We didn't hear the bell. I'm sure it's Simon Welkin."

Aunt Nell's lips tightened white. She said, "Hmn," but her jutting relaxed.

"Is Great-grandfather coming?" asked John again.

"He's looking for something, which I think he will find soon." Aunt Nell gazed at John. "Perhaps you should talk to him later. You're a clever boy, John. You may even take after Great-grandfather. No one else ever has."

SLAPPING THE WALL

Maggie, John and Aunt Nell picnicked under the crab apple trees close to the stream.

Aunt Nell's gooseberry jam attracted bluebottles, and Maggie would have attacked the bluebottles except John said they had a right to live, just like everybody else; so Maggie ladled jam onto a saucer (before covering the main jam with a napkin), and invited the flies to join the picnic.

When the lemonade was finished and the sandwiches were finished and the ramekin and frangipane were finished, and the galantine, pralines, lobscouse and salmagundi were finished, John lay back on the grass, hands behind his head, knees up, staring among the crab apples at the toppling tower.

He waved away a buzzing fly.

SOUND, John remembered Great-grandfather saying, *is an important tool in magic.*

So if Simon Welkin was stealing sound – and he certainly seemed to be – John crinkled his eyes at the sun – anything could happen.

"I think we should clear up!" squealed Maggie. "It's getting very bluebottly!"

So they cleared up, and John went to speak to Great-grandfather Harris.

"I don't want to go!" Maggie stumped towards the ruined cottage.

"Great-grandfather says it's only right."

John stared at the cottage window, but there was no turnip head. "It's our responsibility. At least – it's Great-grandfather's, but he can't go. Stop. There's a fly in your hair."

"Get it out! Yug!"

"It's gone."

They jogged past the ruined cottage; they strolled past pairs of cottages leaning on each other like very old people; they wandered past several cottages stuck together like a cottage sandwich; they dawdled past the new church built only two hundred years ago. They ran along a lane with a horse walking towards them in a field. The horse nodded over the roadside fence, saying "Humph."

"It's a horsy Nellie!" pouted Maggie, and brushed flies from its nose.

The lane wobbled with heat as they sauntered on.

"That must be Toolshed's byre," said John.

"Washed clean by Simon Welkin."

They strode to the farmhouse door and

knocked. A pair of wellingtons lay dead on the step.

"Hello!" A man lumbered from the byre behind them, batting flies with his palm.

"Hello, Mr Tomshed."

"Hello, you two. Down for the holidays?"

"Yes."

"Come into the house. Young Dirk's putting the kettle on."

Mr Tomshed perched on a window-sill and eased free of his wellingtons. A bluebottle hummed around his steamy feet.

"I expect you could manage a slice of cake?"

"We've just had a picnic – "

"Oh, we could!" cried Maggie. "Thank you so much!"

In they went, Mr Tomshed's feet leaving damp prints on the kitchen's stone floor.

Dirk Tomshed – also in his socks, and with jeans covering his legs – was kneeling on a sideboard, slapping at the wall with a newspaper club.

DARKENED GLASS

"Bluebottles!" said Dirk Tomshed. He clambered off the sideboard. "What do you two want? They having tea, Dad? You want tea? My mum made cake. You want cake?"

"Stop prattling, young Dirk," said his father, "and stir up an extra cup or two. Put the newspaper in the bin. I'll just wash my hands."

He lathered at the sink, pausing to shut the window above the taps. He rapped another bluebottle flat with his knuckles, rinsed and towelled, smiling in his big square face.

"Wife's off shopping," he said, "so we give ourselves an extra cuppa. How's your grandad keeping? Marvellous old chap. You know – " He waved John and Maggie to the table and they sat round while Dirk poured, and sugar appeared in a sugar bag, and milk in a jug. " – when I was a boy, your grandad was an old man. Least, that's how he seemed to us kids. Old Man Harris. Half the height of me at Dirk's age. And my father saying he remembered your grandad as an old man when he was a boy. Dare say it was your grandad's dad and my dad was confused, though I remember my grandad saying that old man Harris was marvellous for his age and had seemed old to him since he was a kid.

"Take a slab of that cake. If we eat it, Dirk's mother'll moan that she's feeding the five thousand, and if we don't, she'll think it's no good and not bake for a month. Gone shopping she has. Told you that, didn't I?"

"Excuse me," said John, not really wanting to interrupt but – "Did your grandfather mention someone called Simon Welkin?"

"Simon Welkin. We know that tale, don't we, young Dirk? Dug trenches to make the stream clean out our byre. Cheated – now who was it he cheated? My great great-grandfather's great great-grandfather, I think. They say that's why the old church is shin-deep in the graveyard.

"My great-whatsit grandfather threw tombstones in the stream and fair got his own back. Got the farm back too, of course, else we wouldn't be sitting here, would we? Don't give up a farm to a cheat, do you? Certainly not on a dumb silly bet that nobody with any sense would have taken up in the first place. Getting a bit dark in here, young Dirk? Must be a cloud on the sun. Oh, I remember. Other half of the bet was that Welkin would give his cottage over to my old ancestor if he lost – if

Welkin lost, that is. And of course he did lose cos he cheated, and had to sign his home over to my great-great-you-know.

"Old Tomshed wasn't happy about taking the cottage, but public opinion was for him and against Welkin. So he got the cottage and let it out cheap to whoever needed it and that went on till my Dad's time when dry rot turned the timbers to dust. Young Dirk used to play in it, but not now, eh, young Dirk? Does what his old man says does my Dirk. Place is like to fall down around anybody playing in there, so I've got it locked up. It's getting mighty dark. I hope it don't thunder. Turn the milk, that will – "

"Oh!" said Maggie.

She pointed towards the sink and Mr Tomshed and Dirk twisted in their seats to look.

John frowned.

Maggie said, "Someone's put a sheet of black polythene over your window!"

"Well!" said Mr Tomshed. "Now who'd do a thing like that? And you two – " He smiled at John and Maggie. " – so busy listening to my prattling that you didn't notice. What's that buzzing? You hear it? You hear it, young Dirk? It's pretty loud. I do believe it's been going on for some time." He pushed back his chair, but Maggie was on her feet and dashing to the sink.

She peered at the darkened glass.

"The polythene's moving. That's queer."

John didn't ask what was queer. He stood up.

Maggie leaned over the sink towards the window.

"It's not ordinary polythene. It's shimmery, like – OH!"

John took a step around the table.

"OH JOHN! IT'S NOT POLYTHENE! OH! HOW AWFUL! OH! JOHN! IT'S BLUEBOTTLES!"

CHEWING BLUEBOTTLES

Maggie shrank from the window, and rushed to John.

"Bluebottles!" said Mr Tomshed. He leaned towards the glass, then stepped closer. "I've never seen anything like that."

The buzzing surged and the room darkened.

"The other windows!" gasped John, and everybody gaped across the kitchen at black splodges spreading on the outside of the glass.

"Here, young Dirk!" cried Mr Tomshed, "touch that light switch! That's better."

John thought Mr Tomshed was about to tell them what to do, but the farmer just turned from window to window, silent with astonishment.

"It's Simon Welkin!" squealed Maggie.

"Simon Welkin?" said Mr Tomshed.

"Great-grandfather," said John, "said to warn you that Simon Welkin meant mischief."

"Don't be daft," said Dirk.

"No need for that, young Dirk," said Mr Tomshed. "Your grandad been up to his tricks?"

"I'm afraid so," said John.

"Us kids used to say Old Man Harris could waken the dead. These flies are Welkin's doing?"

"I think so. Aunt Nell's bell lost its sound this morning, and Maggie too. Great-grandfather says sound is basic in magic and Simon Welkin needs it for…" John shrugged. "…conjuring bluebottles?"

"Dad." Dirk Tomshed, standing by the light switch, listened at a door. "I think they're in the hall."

John and Maggie crowded with Mr Tomshed, their ears to the door panels.

"You're right, young Dirk," breathed Mr Tomshed. "Mother must've opened the parlour window. Them brutes are all through the house. I've got to get you kids out of here."

"They can't do us any harm, Dad. Them two, though – " He stared at John and Maggie. " – got to go home."

"That's good thinking, young Dirk," said Mr Tomshed, "but if those bluebottles get in here, there won't be room to breathe. Not to mention being a touch unpleasant."

"Wouldn't bother me," said Dirk.

"I fancy it might," said his father, "chewing bluebottles at every breath."

"Ooh!" wailed Maggie.

"I ain't scared," mumbled Dirk.

"Now don't be foolish, young Dirk. And

talk properly. What would your mother say to hear careless talk like that?"

"Well, I ain't. Amn't. Am not."

"He's a good lad," said Mr Tomshed, but his heavy face frowned and his socks wiggled as his toes tapped thoughtfully.

Mr Tomshed's socks were plain yellow. John looked at Dirk's feet, bigger even than Aunt Nell's. His socks were yellow too, but with a pattern of dark blobs.

Sometimes it takes a second to realize what you are looking at.

It took John two seconds.

For another one second he gazed at the blobs walking on Dirk Tomshed's socks.

For another bit of a second he watched more blobs crawling from under the door and walking about the kitchen's stone floor.

John pulled Maggie back.

The blobs buzzed, rising around Dirk's legs.

MAKING PAPER LEGS

Dirk Tomshed danced. "I hate them bluebottles!" he gasped.

Mr Tomshed stamped, and flapped his hands.

Maggie ran to the bin for the newspaper. John dragged a rug from under the table's feet, and while Maggie clubbed and Dirk danced and Mr Tomshed flapped, John rolled up the rug and stuffed it against the bottom of the door.

"Well done, young John!" said Mr Tomshed.

And they spent the next few minutes – rather uselessly, thought John – batting the few bluebottles that hummed around the kitchen.

Then Mr Tomshed said, "We have to get out. You kids got any ideas?"

"I don't want to go out!" said Maggie.

"I ain't scared," mumbled Dirk.

"We'd have to cover our faces," said John.

"And our legs!" cried Maggie, rubbing her brown skin as if flies were already gathering. "I couldn't stand them on me!"

"There's a pile of old newspapers under the sink," said Dirk.

"Now there's good thinking," said Mr Tomshed. "What do we do with old newspapers?"

"She could tie them round her legs. And him. Ball of twine in the drawer."

"Right. Ri-ight! Well done, my lad. What about our faces?"

"They mustn't get in my hair!" gasped Maggie.

"Sacks in the larder, ain't they?" said Dirk. "What the potatoes were in."

"Potatoes?" Maggie looked at John.

"Better than flies in your hair," said John. "Will we be able to see?"

"Think so." Dirk rummaged in the larder and hauled sacks onto the kitchen floor. "We got enough. Bit dusty." He dropped a sack over his head. It hung down to his hips. "I can see through it. Atchoo!" He pulled the sack off, his eyes watering. "These would do, Dad. Atchoo!"

"Well done, young Dirk. Here's the twine for you kids. Scissors to cut it. Newspaper. Let's shake some dust out of these sacks."

When the paper legs were tied on, John and Maggie walked around to see they didn't pop open.

"You've enough string round you," said Mr Tomshed, "to sink the Queen Mary."

John helped Maggie into her sack. Mr Tomshed helped John. John watched through his sack as Mr Tomshed and Dirk turned into upside-down bags of potatoes.

"Hold the edge of the sack tight, Maggie," said John, "so the flies can't get inside. I think I'm ready. Atchoo!"

"I'm ready," said Dirk.

"Hold my hand, John," whispered Maggie.

"I can't. Stay close behind me, and when I run, you run."

"We'll go out the door we came in," said Mr Tomshed. "No point going through the hall and having two doors to open. Young Dirk, you go first, cos you ain't scared and know the way. Next, you kids. And I'll come last. Line up then. That's it. What a din these little buzzers are kicking up."

"I'll open the door," said Dirk. "Ready?"

THE HORRIBLE WAR

John felt Maggie at his back. He heard Dirk panting through his sack.

The door clacked open wide! and flies hosed in. Black! Instantly, John couldn't see. Maggie screamed. Dirk yelled. Mr Tomshed gasped, "Run!"

"Run!" shrieked John, and he ran, head-down blind with bluebottles, straight forward, hoping he wouldn't trip on Dirk. He howled to guide Maggie. He pictured where the byre was. He didn't want to run into the wall. He veered towards the lane – he hoped. He screwed tight the edge of the sack with one hand and patted the inside with the other to knock away the flies. He could see.

Along the lane he ran. "Stop!" he yelled.

He threw off the sack and dragged away Maggie's, swiping at bluebottles.

Mr Tomshed ran blindly and they shouted. He stopped and pushed up his sack. "You kids all right? You're shuddering."

Maggie and John nodded.

"Where's Dirk?"

John looked around. "He was in front of me. He must be along the lane. Dirk! Dirk!"

"Dirk!" screamed Maggie. "Oh, look at the farmhouse! You don't think he's still inside!"

The farmhouse walls were a black fuzz. A strange bush seemed to grow out of the open doorway, but the bush was flies, rushing into the kitchen. Even in the lane, their buzzing roared in John's ears.

"DIRK!" bellowed Mr Tomshed, but no Dirk appeared down the lane.

"You can't go back in!" shouted Maggie as Mr Tomshed pulled on his sack.

The big farmer ran. He ran into the black bush. Its buzzing surged horribly. The bush gobbled him up.

"What can we do!" Tears made rivers on Maggie's face.

Panic jerked through John.

"Do something!" screamed Maggie.

John patted the pockets of his shorts. He had nothing. Wait a second. What's this? A screw he hadn't used for the sundial. That's no use. He dropped it. Here's something else. Flat and square. What – ? A book of matches.

"Dirk's matches," said John. "I must have put them in my pocket when I was in the ruined cottage."

Maggie stared at the matches. "Can't we use them? Set fire to the flies?"

John looked for Mr Tomshed and Dirk, but he saw only the bush buzzing horribly in the doorway.

"We need something to burn to chase the flies away," he said. "Pick up your sack! Come on! Oh, come on! You can't be a scaredy cat now! Mr Tomshed and Dirk are in there! They won't be able to breathe!"

So they ran, Maggie's feet stumping on the lane, John hauling her towards the byre.

Giant rolls of hay stood about the byre entrance. Mr Tomshed's tractor rested in the sunlight, a coil of rope tucked behind its seat.

"What can we do!" cried Maggie.

"I don't know! Let me think!"

John stared around. Dirk had been in the kitchen a long time. He remembered there were two doors to the kitchen: the one they'd just come out, and the one into the hall. And the hall would lead to the front door of the farmhouse.

"Maggie."

"What?"

"Get that rope off the tractor!" John ran around the rolls of hay. Most of them were taller than he was. He found one that was shoulder-high and leaned on its curved side. "It's moving! Help me! Push it towards the farmhouse! Towards the kitchen door!"

"What will you do!"

"Heave! It's rolling! Set it on fire! Don't let it roll away!"

"But it will block the doorway!"

"There's nothing else to burn!" screamed John. "We don't have time to find anything smaller! We'll get Dirk and Mr Tomshed out through the hall! We're in line with the door! Stop! Stop!"

He scraped a match and pressed it into the hairy curve of the roll. Hay crackled. Flames danced almost invisible in the bright daylight.

"Push!"

Smoke burst in all direction as the roll trundled towards the doorway.

"The rolling's putting the flames out!" gasped Maggie.

"It's stuck in the doorway! It's burning! Give me the rope! Get the sacks! Come on! Come on!"

They ran round the farmhouse, John tying an end of the rope about his waist, the sacks flapping in Maggie's grasp. The newspaper was falling from John's legs.

They stopped a few paces from the front door.

"You stay here," said John, "and hold the rope. It'll guide me out. Put your sack on. I hope we're not too late. Right!"

He risked one hand outside the sack, and ran among the bluebottles.

He grasped the doorhandle. Flies burst on his palm.

He turned the handle, and pushed.

He pushed again.

This was the only way into the kitchen, the only way to get Dirk and Mr Tomshed out.

But the door was locked.

SOCKS IN JELLY

John panicked.

He kicked the door and screamed. Bluebottles buzzed around him and he didn't care. They clambered on his hand. He thudded his foot against the door. They bumbled inside his sack. It was only when flies' feet touched his screaming lips that he turned from the door, gasping, struggling out of the sack, saying, "Ooooh! Uh! Ugh! Yug! Maggie! Maggie! What can we do!" Then –

"They're out!" said Maggie.

John gaped. Mr Tomshed and Dirk sprawled on the earth – sacks flung aside – socks stained with red jelly that was trodden-on flies, Mr Tomshed patting Dirk's knee, Dirk, white-faced like a block of cheese.

"How did you get out!" shouted John.

"Back parlour window," gasped Mr Tomshed. "I knew our Mother had left it open. Your smoke fairly helped, young John. Dropping like flies in there, they were. Not that the smoke's much fun, but easier to handle for my lad than them bluebottles."

"The hay will still be burning!"

"Good thinking, young John, but don't go dashing about. There's a fire extinguisher in the milking shed. You're looking a bit peaky. I'll go."

And he trotted off to save his house.

"The buzzing's louder!" said John.

"Are there more coming?" cried Maggie.

Dirk scrambled up.

"They're going!" cried John. "We've beaten them! Look! They're flying away!"

And they looked, and the great buzzing was the fuzz leaving the farmhouse, darkening the sky, then vanishing. And the farmhouse was normal except for splashes on the door where John's feet had squashed flies, and except – "What *is* that?" demanded Maggie – the white walls were brown, and a column of smoke stirred from around the corner into the brilliant sky.

"Fly droppings," said John. "Making the walls brown. A thousand million fly droppings." Then they went to help Mr Tomshed move the roll of hay.

Maggie and John sat in Aunt Nell's kitchen sipping cocoa touched with honey, flavoured with stirred-in spices. No one made cocoa like Aunt Nell!

The afternoon sun reached in the window and stroked Maggie's damp hair. John's face tingled and his fingers wobbled like prunes on sticks after being scrubbed in the bath by Aunt Nell. ("If you are YOUNG ENOUGH to get this DIRTY, you are YOUNG ENOUGH for me to BATH YOU!")

"The worst bit," John told Aunt Nell as she pulled apple pie from the oven and placed it on the table, "was burning the flies. After we'd swept them into the yard – "

"Twillions of them!" breathed Maggie.

"They were ankle deep in the kitchen," agreed John.

"Dirk was so brave," sighed Maggie, "without his wellingtons."

"We came home then," grinned John, "and paddled in the stream to clean our sand-shoes."

"Where you caught us," sighed Maggie to Aunt Nell. "Wasn't Dirk brave? After what he suffered? Trapped in the house. Escaping through the smoke, then actually sweeping those horrid bluebottles from the kitchen in his dear yellow socks..."

John squawked with laughter.

Maggie gazed into her cocoa.

Aunt Nell's glance descended on Maggie and one eyebrow rose.

"You must tell Great-grandfather," said Aunt Nell.

John looked at her.

"It's not over," said his aunt. "You don't think this is the end? Now that you have helped the Tomsheds, Simon Welkin's revenge will be on us all."

FALL DOWN SCREAMING

John told Great-grandfather about the bluebottles, then he was surprised to hear a car *toot! toot!* outside the church.

John dashed to the door, Maggie at his back, meeting Aunt Nell as she pulled the door open and tramped up a step or two to see who was tooting.

John raised his eyebrows at a woman marching along the path with Mr Tomshed pleading behind her, and Dirk scuffing along like the cow's tail.

The woman, thought John, was very angry. Poor Great-grandfather was about to be blamed for Simon Welkin's mischief.

"Why," cried Aunt Nell, "it's dear Mrs Tomshed!"

Maggie goggled up at John. Aunt Nell was *never* so friendly!

"Oh, do come in!" Aunt Nell's arm swept the air aside to allow Mrs Tomshed through the hall. "And Mr Tomshed! And Dirk! How nice to see you!"

Mrs Tomshed's face twisted around her mouth.

"Into the kitchen!" cried Aunt Nell. "We'll boil up the kettle! Apple pie! If these two monkeys of mine have left any! Your mother makes excellent apple pie, eh, Dirk? Better than Harrods'. Ha! Ha! Sit down, sit down. Mine won't be up to your standard, Mrs Tomshed – "

John saw Maggie sag with disbelief.

" – but some fresh cream from your very own cows will cover any mistakes. The kettle won't be a moment. You're all looking a bit weary. The children were telling me about your trouble. How awful! How dreadful! I do sympathize! I remember when two crows came in here... You'll manage a LARGE slice of apple pie? You must be hungry. Why, you won't be able to cook in your kitchen tonight! You must stay to tea! Don't shake your head – " Aunt Nell's hand raised itself to silence Mrs Tomshed's head-shaking. " – I insist. Some of the responsibility is mine, on behalf of Great-grandfather – "

John sagged beside Maggie.

" – and I will do everything possible to help. You mustn't thank me! There! The kettle's boiling. Eat up! John, fetch the cream from the fridge, my dear."

Maggie mouthed *my dear!* and John swallowed a squawk as he rushed to the fridge.

"There's boiled ham for tea," said Aunt Nell. "Home-grown potatoes, sautéd, I think, then deep-fried. Beetroot from the garden. Lettuce, chives and radishes... Oh, Maggie, darling, do pull me two nice lettuces – not the dark green ones, my sweet – and radishes. And take the scissors to cut the chives – "

"I'll help!" gasped John.

"Thank you, my darlings!" called Aunt Nell, as John fled with Maggie through the hall, out the front door because it was the nearest way into outside – and Maggie screamed and fell beside the path, lunatic laughter startling crows in the tower, John cackling so much that the duck came waddling to investigate...

Oh, dear.

Oh, Aunt Nell.

Phew.

"Ha! Ha! Ha!" sighed John.

"Golly-cripes," groaned Maggie.

Far away, near where the stream arose from a hillside, lightning danced between the sky and the earth.

NOT THUNDERY
SORT OF WEATHER

"Come on, Maggie," gasped John. "Radishes, my sweet. Lettuce and chives, my darlings."

"Don't!" sighed Maggie.

They chortled around the garden, Maggie using her shirt-front as a basket for the vegetables, John gazing at the distant hill.

"I *thought* I saw lightning," he said. "Listen. One, two..."

"Lightning?"

"Listen. Three, four..."

"But it's blistering hot!"

"Seven, eight..."

"Oh, it's not going to rain!"

"Eleven..."

Maggie waited, the vegetables bulging in her pulled-up shirt.

"Nineteen, twenty..."

Thunder whispered across the fields.

"It's very far away," said John.

"But it's not thundery sort of weather!" complained Maggie.

"No," agreed John, and led Maggie back to the church.

"I was JUST SAYING, my dears," boomed Aunt Nell as John and Maggie entered the kitchen, "that you won't mind giving up your bedroom to Mr and Mrs Tomshed – not at all, Mrs Tomshed! There's another room further up the tower for the children, and Dirk can share – "

"Share!" squealed Maggie and dropped the vegetables onto the gravestones. "I'm a girl!"

"Dirk won't mind, will you, Dirk? There! More tea? Apple pie finished? Dirk and Mr Tomshed are off now to milk their cows. Open the door for Mr Tomshed, John. And Mrs Tomshed will phone professional cleaners to clean the farmhouse first thing tomorrow – at Great-grandfather's expense! I insist. Teatime in two hours! John and Maggie, move your things into the upper room, my darlings. Clear the kitchen! Your aunt has FOOD TO PREPARE!"

"Move out of our room!" groaned John as he clattered up the iron stairs.

Maggie's heels flashed at his face. "*I will not share with Pigshed!*" she screamed.

She flung open the bedroom door and marched to her bed. She thumped onto it, scowling.

"I thought you fancied him," grinned John. "Shove everything into the suitcase."

"I only admired his *socks!*"

Maggie glowered out the window. "It's hot!" She levered the window open. "I can see clouds above the hill. And lightning."

John counted to fourteen.

Rumble, said the thunder.

"It's closer," he said.

"It still doesn't *feel* thundery."

John threw his pyjamas into the case. "No, it doesn't," he said solemnly.

Maggie turned from the window and looked at him.

"What do you mean?" she asked.

John shrugged and found Maggie's slippers. "Catch."

Maggie caught one slipper and let the other hit the floor.

Her eyes saucered at him. "You don't think…?"

John raised his eyebrows.

"You do," whispered Maggie. "You think it's him! First flies and now thunder! *You think it's Simon Welkin, don't you!*"

LIGHTNING!

John stood beside his sundial watching lightning stand between the clouds and the countryside.

He could hear Aunt Nell's voice and Mrs Tomshed's replies through the open kitchen window as the ladies washed and dried after the evening meal.

Clouds had approached during teatime, darkening the landscape.

Now lightning jagged down. In five seconds thunder grumbled across the garden.

Raindrops rolled dust from the rhubarb, and the fruit trees rattled as rain dropped through their branches. Dark splashes appeared on the rocks in the river-bed.

A roar made John stare upstream.

He said, "Wow!" For among the trees sped a shining monster.

Its mouth boiled with foam, and its wet body filled the river-bed. Boulders tumbled as the monster swept downstream. Weeds tore free from the banks and spun inside its body.

John realized that a lot of rain must have fallen miles upstream for such a monster of water to come rushing past the garden now.

Rain beat on John's hair, and he ran and stood under the door's arch at the bottom of the brick steps. Peter Pan nodded his flowery heads, and John tapped his toe on the metal grid that separated the steps from the house. Water ran through the grid's holes into a drain. Beside the steps, crumbs of soil trickled onto the grid.

John retreated into the house and shut the door on the weather.

He passed a pair of very dirty shoes, large enough to fit Dirk, standing on a newspaper in the hall.

In the kitchen, Maggie and Dirk (Dirk in his jellied yellow socks) watched Mr Tomshed's nodding fists as he explained the art of hand-milking.

Mrs Tomshed and Aunt Nell discussed puddings.

John watched the sky darken beyond the kitchen windows.

"Maggie, my darling!" cried Aunt Nell. "Please put on the light!"

Dirk reached the switch first and raised his hand to it.

Lightning flared.

"Perhaps you shouldn't touch the switch, young Dirk," said Mr Tomshed. "That lightning could come rushing through the wires – "

"I am not scared," said Dirk carefully.
"Now, young Dirk – "
Dirk thumbed the switch.
Lightning turned the kitchen white.
Dirk yelped.
Once.

A BEDFUL OF TOMSHEDS

Mr Tomshed clawed the table as he stood up.

John said, "What's wrong, Dirk?"

Dirk leaned one hand on Aunt Nell's kitchen wall and looked at his foot with the other.

"My sock's wet," he said. "There's a puddle on the floor."

"Come on!" said John.

They followed a trickle of water across the hall. "It's coming under the front door!" cried John.

He remembered the earth crumbling onto the grid. Perhaps more earth had fallen. "Maybe the drain's blocked."

He opened the door, and thought that the giant had returned, because the door heaved inwards with a thrust that knocked him against Maggie.

Earth avalanched through the doorway. Water spread on the tiles, hurrying towards the kitchen, bobbing Dirk's shoes off the newspaper.

Outside, rain fell fiercely.

"What's up, young Dirk? Oh!" said Mr

Tomshed staring from the kitchen. "Let's have that door shut!" He splashed forward but more earth sluiced down until the doorway was blocked higher than John's head, and mud, stones and plants pushed half-across the hall.

"We must get out of this," said Mr Tomshed. "Ladies!" he shouted, "we must go up the stairs! Come on, young Maggie, young John, young Dirk! Follow me! Keep calm – "

They clattered up the iron steps and onto the unsloped floor of the bedroom.

Mr Tomshed and Mrs Tomshed waltzed downhill (it seemed) holding each other, until they toppled onto John's bed. Dirk clung to a wardrobe, feeling the air with a socky foot, and all three cried out in surprise using strange farming words.

Lightning threw shadows about the room.

John stared from a window. A flash crackled down the ash tree. Smoke burst from the tree's roots, then steam; and the tree groaned, leaning towards the river. Then it plunged between the river's banks, and water surged over the garden.

"Aunt Nell!" gasped John. "We've forgotten Great-grandfather!"

From the hall, rose Aunt Nell's voice, demanding.

Great-grandfather's thin replies twisted up the staircase.

"How are they coming so quickly!" said Maggie. "Great-grandfather's slower than a hedgehog!"

John and Maggie watched the door curiously.

"You must try!" ordered Aunt Nell, and Great-grandfather's head came round the door, face up to the ceiling, rust-coloured wig dangling on its blob of paste.

Aunt Nell stepped backwards into the room, carrying Great-grandfather Harris in her arms.

"Simon Welkin is too strong," Great-grandfather was saying, "for me to send him away."

"Great-grandfather."

"Yes, John?"

Aunt Nell balanced Great-grandfather on his feet, then almost knocked him over by tidying his blue velvet jacket.

"I've got an idea." John glanced at the L.N.E.R. clock. "May I whisper it, Great-grandfather?"

"Of course, John. Quiet, everyone, please."

"Nobody's making a noise, Great-grandfather," said Maggie.

"You're perfectly right, Maggie," said Great-grandfather. "Tell me, John. Yes. Yes. I don't see why not. Stand back, my darlings."

John pulled Maggie (who had crept close to listen) away from Great-grandfather.

"SIMON WELKIN!" Great-grandfather's old voice rang above the drumming of the rain. "WE WOULD MAKE A BET WITH YOU!"

The drumming faded to a patter.

"It's the sort of bet you like, old friend. Not much risk."

The patter ceased.

"I thought that would catch him," murmured Great-grandfather. "A child's game, Simon. We'll play hide and seek, you and I. In this room. You go away for five minutes while I hide, then you must find me in two minutes. If you lose – " Great-grandfather paused as something invisible rattled across the ceiling. "If you lose, you return to where you came from. Do you accept?"

The rattling fled excitedly around the walls, then it struck twice, like a question.

"Ah," said Great-grandfather. "If you win..." He blinked up at John. "If he wins...?"

"Whether he WINS or whether he LOSES!" boomed Aunt Nell, before John could speak, "this is his chance to be remembered AS A MAN WHO DOES NOT CHEAT!"

Silence rose, like a threat.

"Aunt Nell's right!" shouted John desperately. "People say terrible things about you! Don't you want to change that? Go on!

Go away for five minutes while Great-grandfather hides!"

The threat lessened.

The silence filled with emptiness.

"Well done, John," gasped Great-grandfather.

John leapt down the iron staircase.

He splashed through the hall and up the brass steps into Great-grandfather's room.

He ran to the box of tricks and hauled aside the lion's skin. He flung back the lid and pulled out Maggie's golden cloak and red hat.

Then the silver cloak.

Then the witch's hat.

More cloaks and hats followed until the box was empty.

John felt into the wooden corners.

The blackest-cloak-that-ever-was, *wasn't!*

John threw himself across the room.

Great-grandfather Harris had been sitting on the African stool with his back to the fire, when Aunt Nell had barged in. He had dropped the cloak behind him.

John felt along the hearth.

Something soft filled his palm.

"Got you!" he whispered.

THE DANCING WARDROBES

John burst into the bedroom. "Hurry, Great-grandfather!"

"Where have you been!" shrieked Maggie. "There's only a minute left!"

Great-grandfather gathered himself into the cloak and pulled up the hood. Just a flicker of a slipper showed as John guided him to the gloomy place where the chair waited between the wardrobes.

John hurried to Aunt Nell. Maggie goggled at the chair.

The rattling clattered, making everyone jump.

The cover on Maggie's bed billowed then flattened.

The Chinese screen crashed to the floor.

The doors of the wardrobes flew open and clothes streamed out.

The rattling rushed to every corner of the room and back again.

"Twenty seconds to go!" gasped John.

The rattle battered angrily, returning to the

wardrobes as if it suspected Great-grandfather's presence.

Aunt Nell took a tiny step towards the chair. John hung on her wrist.

"Ten seconds!" John stared at the clock. "Nine!"

The wardrobes danced like mad things. John held grimly to Aunt Nell's arm.

"Six!" he panted.

The wardrobes squashed the chair.

"*Don't move, Aunt Nell! Five!*"

"Four!" yelped Maggie. "Three, Great-grandfather! Two!"

The chair split along its seat.

"One – !"

The seat burst as the wardrobes slammed together, and pieces of the chair leapt about the room.

"Zero!" gasped John.

The rattling sped across the ceiling. A window crashed open and glass fell out of the frame.

"He's gone!" cried Maggie. "But *where's Great-grandfather!*"

"Here I am, my darlings."

Great-grandfather Harris appeared out of his cloak, standing close to Aunt Nell.

" I thought I'd hide in your shadow, Nell," said Great-grandfather, "just in case someone stared at the chair."

"Oh, I didn't!" howled Maggie.

"Of course not, Maggie."

"I glimpsed the toe of your slipper, Great-grandfather," said John, "when you walked towards Aunt Nell."

"I'm glad you did, John." Great-grandfather patted Aunt Nell's hand. "John held onto you, Nell, so you wouldn't step away and leave me exposed. You'll be glad to hear that I have found what I was looking for." He shook John's hand as if meeting him for the first time.

"And now, I'm rather tired. Pick me up, Nell. Don't bump my head on the wall. Goodbye, Mrs Tomshed, Mr Tomshed. Goodbye Dirk… Watch you don't slip on the stairs, Nell. Perhaps Mr Tomshed would oblige us by digging away the mud from the front door so we can shut it. I'm feeling quite chilly…"

OUTSIDE

John and Maggie splashed bare-foot from a kitchen window into the garden.

The rhubarb drooped, half under water. Simon Welkin's card table shone damply in the evening sun. The duck paddled around the sundial quacking with delight at having a lake to swim in.

Mr Tomshed and Dirk clambered from the kitchen window carrying spades. They disappeared down the brick steps, and the sound of digging joined the plop of rain-water dripping from the fruit trees.

John and Maggie paddled across the garden to stare at the toppled ash tree with the river hurrying through its branches.

John glanced towards the village. "Look, Maggie," he said. "The cottage roof has fallen in. Lightning must've struck it. That really is the finish of Simon Welkin."

He peered at the upstairs window of the cottage, startled for a second, as something stared from behind the glass. Then he saw it was only rubble stacked inside the room.

He said, "Hah," in a sigh.

John was happy that Great-grandfather had found what he was looking for. Funny how he had shaken John's hand as if in welcome.

John had a sudden picture of himself scratching the numbers for the sundial. And rolling the fiery hay at the Tomsheds' kitchen. Then finally, telling Great-grandfather his idea for beating Simon Welkin.

John smiled. Aunt Nell had said that he took after Great-grandfather. Great-grandfather, John realized with a shock of delight, had been looking for *him*.

He watched Maggie wading behind the duck. Her hair flowed golden in the sunlight. She was encouraging the duck's swimming by patting its bottom.

John thought she moved differently; more grown-up.

She really had faced the bluebottles.

John paddled towards the steps where the Tomsheds were digging mud from the hall.

Great-grandfather would be waiting, to share with him, the secrets of the box of tricks.

He gazed back at his sister. He didn't really want to spoil her happiness that their adventure was ended. But he couldn't resist.

"Maggie!" he said above the thud of spades.

She looked round.

John beamed.

"We still have to sleep with Toolshed."

THE GARGOYLE

Hugh Scott

"No! No! No! You don't understand! The fear will kill you!"

On first sight, the new Scottish home of Professor Kent and his family seems quite idyllic. But there's a chill about the place that's not simply due to snow – an atmosphere of menace that young Marion, with her psychic powers, quickly senses. It seems to have something to do with the mysterious German and a boy called Callum who live in the nearby castle. Before long, Marion and her father find themselves in a tense battle of wits and wills – a life and death struggle that brings them face to face with the terrifying gargoyle…

"Followers of Hugh Scott will relish the mannered deliberation with which menace builds up in *The Gargoyle*."
The Independent

"The kind of book that once you start you've got to finish. You can't possibly put it down for another sitting. It moves at a pretty cracking pace."
BBC Radio's Treasure Islands

MORE WALKER PAPERBACKS
For You to Enjoy

☐ 0-7445-2330-3   *The Gargoyle*
by Hugh Scott   £3.99

☐ 0-7445-3680-4   *The Place Between*
by Hugh Scott   £3.99

☐ 0-7445-2308-7   *Something Watching*
by Hugh Scott   £3.99

☐ 0-7445-5215-X   *A Ghost Waiting*
by Hugh Scott   £3.99

☐ 0-7445-5216-8   *The Haunted Sand*
by Hugh Scott   £3.99

☐ 0-7445-4794-6   *The Camera Obscura*
by Hugh Scott   £3.99

☐ 0-7445-2040-1   *Why Weeps the Brogan?*
by Hugh Scott   £3.99

Name _____

Address _____

_____